THE HARDY BOYS™
SECRET-CODE
ACTIVITY BOOK

By Tony Tallarico With Text by Nancy T. Rockwell

Based on Hardy Boys™ Mystery Stories by Franklin W. Dixon

Publishers · GROSSET & DUNLAP · New York
A FILMWAYS COMPANY

FLIGHT BY CARAVAN

Nyree Marshall, an important witness in an international spy case, is in danger. The Hardys have been assigned the task of protecting her.

With Nyree, Joe and Frank join a gypsy caravan and travel incognito from city to city, where the gypsies have carnivals and give shows. In each city, the boys must contact an agent in case Nyree's information is needed.

One day, during a carnival, Frank suspects that Nyree has been recognized, and once again her life is in danger. The three of them must leave the caravan, but first they must let their contact know that they are being followed.

In his last act, Joe plays a hurdy-gurdy while a trained monkey pulls a slip of paper with a fortune out of a box and hands it to spectators. When they pass Joe's contact, he gives the monkey a coded note to deliver.

Can you help the agent read the message so that he can assist Frank, Joe, and Nyree?

SFNEA PESAL ODPVL TEYEY TRMWO EAUIU DTSLX BITLY YOLCZ

KEY:

There are forty-five letters in this code. If you make a grid with nine spaces down and five spaces across, you can insert the first five letters in the first row, then do the same with the second row. To read the message, follow the arrows shown below. The last three letters in the message are called nulls. That is, they have no meaning. They are there so that we can start out with the right number of characters.

S	F	N	E	A
P	E	S	A	L
Q	D	P	V	L
T	E	Y	E	Y
T	R	M	W	O
E	A	U	I	U
D	T	S	L	M
B	I	T	L	N
↓ Y	↓ O	↓ L	C ↓	X ↓

MIDSUMMER NIGHT

Frank, Joe, Chet, Biff, and Tony plan to see a production of *A Midsummer Night's Dream* at the summer-stock repertory theater just outside Bayport. They are thrilled because their friend Joshua Marlborough is scheduled to play the part of Oberon, king of the fairies.

On opening night, however, Joshua does not appear, and the management announces that his understudy will take his place. The boys are disappointed and surprised, since they had spoken with Josh earlier in the day, and they know he was eager to perform.

"I don't understand it," Chet says.

During intermission, the boys go backstage to talk with Josh, but he is not there. The manager is also puzzled.

"He disappeared just before curtain time. He even had his make-up and costume on."

"That's not like him," Joe says.

"I think we'd better look for him," Frank suggests.

While Chet, Biff, and Tony go back to the theater to watch the remainder of the performance, Frank and Joe conduct a search of the buildings in the theater complex.

They walk through an alleyway. As they enter one of the darkened buildings, Joe hears a sound. He turns to look, only to feel himself being pushed inside. He stumbles into Frank, and the two boys fall to the floor. Then the door is closed and locked.

As soon as they get their bearings, Frank and Joe realize that they are not alone. Joshua Marlborough is in the room with them. He is bound and gagged, and what's more, he has been injured.

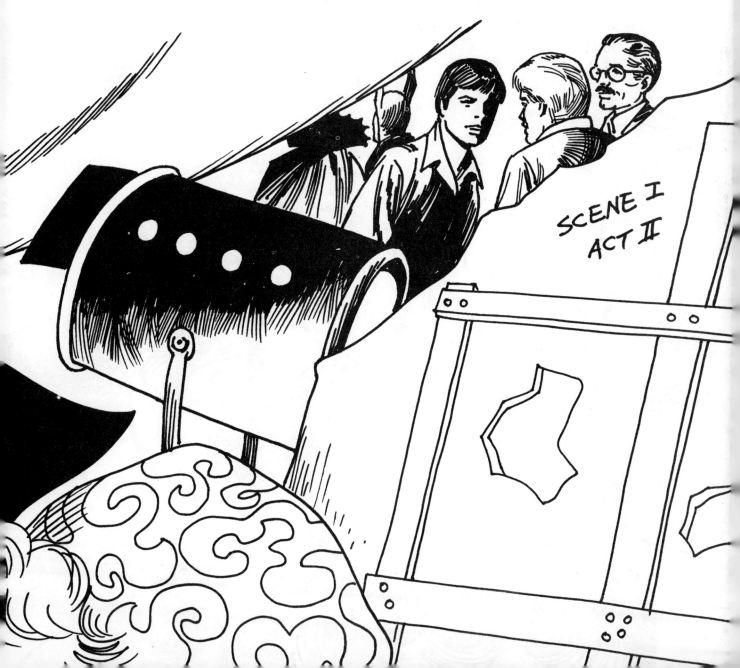

SCENE I
ACT II

"Frank! Joe!" he says. "Thank goodness you're here. They're planning an attempt on the life of Governor Warburton. We must stop them. When I found out, they locked me here in the Smith Building."

"Who?" Frank asks.

"My understudy and an accomplice. They plan to do it after the play, during curtain calls."

Frank and Joe try to attract attention, but no one hears them. "Better write a note," Frank says. "Our friends will be looking for us soon."

"What if the accomplice finds it?" Joe asks.

Frank thinks for a moment. Then he says, "We'll write it in code, tie it in a handkerchief, and throw it into the alley. If the accomplice finds it, he'll just think someone lost a handkerchief. The boys will recognize it."

"Good idea," Joe says. "Better weigh it down with something. Here, use my key."

Can you help Chet, Biff, and Tony read the Hardys' note?

S6 J1 O5 O1 J6 O5 H5 S4 O4 S5   H3 J3 O2 J2   J3 O4   H1 J1 O4 S2 J2 O5
J4 J6 S5 H5   H3 J2 J1 O6 J2   H5 H2 J2 J1 H5 J2 O5
S2 J2 H5   J6 S5 S4 J6 H5 S4 O2 S5 J4 J3 H5 H2   O1 J6 J3 H3 H1 J3 O4 S2

KEY:

	1	2	3	4	5	6	7
J	A	E	I	M	Q	U	Y
O	B	F	J	N	R	V	Z
S	C	G	K	O	S	W	
H	D	H	L	P	T	X	

GREENHOUSE FRONT

Rodney Haversmith has set up a plant nursery in Bayport. Frank and Joe have been in the greenhouse twice, and each time they left feeling uncomfortable.

"I don't know what Haversmith is doing," Frank says. "But I don't trust him."

"His plants look sick," Joe adds. "Did you notice?"

Frank nods. "Maybe it's the people we saw in there. I just don't like their looks."

"Should we mention this to Dad?" Joe asks.

"Yes, but we don't know where he is," Frank answers. "Strange he hasn't been in touch with us." Frank thinks about this for a while.

"There must be a reason for it," Joe says. "Do you remember what he said the last time we talked to him?"

"Yes," Frank murmurs. "He said he was going to see a man with a brown thumb!"

The two boys return to the greenhouse late that night and look around. After searching all over, Joe sees something attached to a bush. It looks like a note. It's from Fenton Hardy, but it's in code. If you were the Hardy boys, would you know what to do?

IMLIN   AODCR   CEEEG   KLDRO   LNEHU   UENSE

KEY:

This is a tricky one. After you put the letters in the grid, you have to read them in the correct order to get the message. Fill in the grid below by putting the first five letters in the first column and filling in the other spaces the same way. The message still doesn't make sense unless you follow the path shown below to read it.

THE LOST SCROLL

Frank and Joe have gone on a trip to the Mideast with Chet, Biff, and Tony. They are on a fascinating assignment to find a papyrus scroll that disappeared from the museum many years before.

"You are my last resort," the curator tells them. "If you can't find it, we don't know who can. We'll just have to give up."

Frank and Joe ask the curator for a complete history of the papyrus, how it was found, who saw it, and what happened to the people who were involved with it.

As the man speaks, the boys get the feeling that the scroll is still somewhere in the museum.

"What happened to the archaeologist who found it?" Frank asks.

"He died," the curator says, "of a strange disease. He knew something would happen to that scroll. He just knew it. He worried about it all the time."

On a hunch the boys ask to be taken to the storerooms of the museum, especially those in which the archaeologist's finds are kept. There they search everything—vases, tapestries, cases of ancient shards, even books. Then Frank picks up an old journal, which gives complete descriptions of the archaeologist's discoveries. At the bottom of the last page, Frank sees a strange series of letters.

"What do you think this means, Joe?" he asks.

Can you help the boys read the entry?

PDORPERYA   LUGIFSUNL   ACURINEEC   CTIONOFVN   EDSCROLLI

KEY:

To decipher this message, write the letters in a grid having nine spaces down and five spaces across. Then put the letters in the spaces. Start with the first group of nine letters, placing them in the first column. Do the same with the others. To read this code, follow the path shown below.

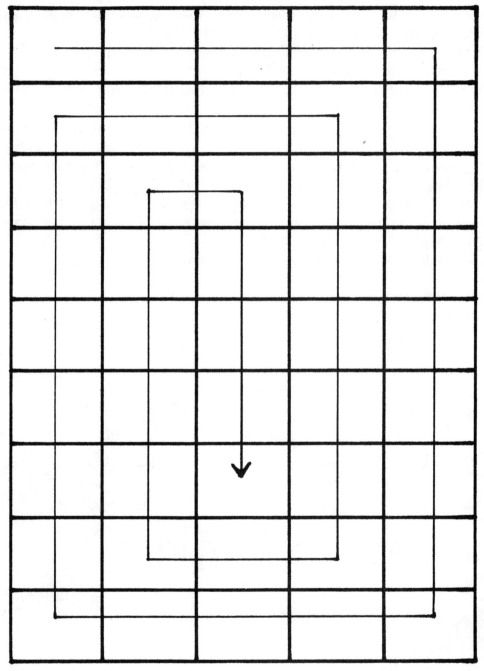

DANGER ON THE SKI SLOPES

Frank, Joe, Biff, Chet, and Tony had been looking forward for weeks to their ski trip, and now it has turned into a nightmare.

On the first day of their vacation, there was an accident on one of the ski lifts. A young woman was seriously injured. Chet and Biff were hurt too. Then the furnace in their lodge broke down, and after that all the skis disappeared during the night.

The boys speak to the manager, who looks worried and frightened. "I'm beginning to think I will sell this place after all," he tells them.

"Has someone been trying to buy it?" Frank asks.

"I keep getting phone calls. Whenever I say I don't want to sell, the caller says, 'We'll see how you feel about it tomorrow.' Then something terrible happens."

The boys investigate. Before long they track down the mysterious caller. He's a man named Oliver Gordon who knows that the lodge and the land it is on will soon triple in value. What's more, the boys learn that Gordon is secretly paying the employees at the lodge to help him sabotage it.

The boys decide it is time to contact Fenton Hardy. They send a telegram, but they want to be sure that Gordon and his accomplices don't find out that the Hardys have learned of their plot.

Can you help Fenton Hardy read the telegram?

TWLOM AIJWBIOML JG OWZLWV
TBEADNTTH QGXQTS
EVVU YVCG KF TCFJV ZE
UXBGZ PTMVAXW

KEY: TRIP

To read this message, rearrange the key word so that it is in alphabetical order—I, P, R, T—then follow the chart below. The first row is the alphabet in its correct sequence. To decipher the first line of the message, look for the code letters in the alphabet beginning with I. Then write down the letters at the top of the column that correspond to cipher letters. For instance, the letter "T" in the I-alphabet corresponds to the letter "L" in the secret message. "W" becomes "O"; "L" is "D"; "O" is "G"; and "M" is "E". To decipher the second, third, and fourth lines, use the alphabets beginning with P, R, and T.

```
A B C D E F G H I J K L M N O P Q R S T U V W X Y Z
B C D E F G H I J K L M N O P Q R S T U V W X Y Z A
C D E F G H I J K L M N O P Q R S T U V W X Y Z A B
D E F G H I J K L M N O P Q R S T U V W X Y Z A B C
E F G H I J K L M N O P Q R S T U V W X Y Z A B C D
F G H I J K L M N O P Q R S T U V W X Y Z A B C D E
G H I J K L M N O P Q R S T U V W X Y Z A B C D E F
H I J K L M N O P Q R S T U V W X Y Z A B C D E F G
I J K L M N O P Q R S T U V W X Y Z A B C D E F G H
J K L M N O P Q R S T U V W X Y Z A B C D E F G H I
K L M N O P Q R S T U V W X Y Z A B C D E F G H I J
L M N O P Q R S T U V W X Y Z A B C D E F G H I J K
M N O P Q R S T U V W X Y Z A B C D E F G H I J K L
N O P Q R S T U V W X Y Z A B C D E F G H I J K L M
O P Q R S T U V W X Y Z A B C D E F G H I J K L M N
P Q R S T U V W X Y Z A B C D E F G H I J K L M N O
Q R S T U V W X Y Z A B C D E F G H I J K L M N O P
R S T U V W X Y Z A B C D E F G H I J K L M N O P Q
S T U V W X Y Z A B C D E F G H I J K L M N O P Q R
T U V W X Y Z A B C D E F G H I J K L M N O P Q R S
U V W X Y Z A B C D E F G H I J K L M N O P Q R S T
V W X Y Z A B C D E F G H I J K L M N O P Q R S T U
W X Y Z A B C D E F G H I J K L M N O P Q R S T U V
X Y Z A B C D E F G H I J K L M N O P Q R S T U V W
Y Z A B C D E F G H I J K L M N O P Q R S T U V W X
Z A B C D E F G H I J K L M N O P Q R S T U V W X Y
```

THE GREAT WHALE HUNT

The Hardys have been asked to join a research crew on the Pacific seaboard, where whales have been beaching themselves and dying. But there is another reason why the Hardys have been asked to go along. The captain of the *Sea Bird* knows that someone has been illegally killing whales in the Pacific. Since these sea creatures are an endangered species, the captain wants the killers apprehended, and he thinks the Hardys can help.

A short while after the boys join the crew, they realize that the ship's radio operator signals the location of whales to a waiting fishing boat in return for a percentage of the profits.

After a brief consultation with the captain, Frank and Joe decide to contact their dad so that they can apprehend all of the law-breakers. They don't want to alert the radio operator.

The boys finally flag down a passing ship and give the captain a note to pass on to their dad, who is waiting for word from them at the San Francisco piers.

Maybe you can help Mr. Hardy break the code.

13. 14. 28. 26. 21. 24. 11. 10. 9. 11. 28. 20. 17. 10. 24. 28
27. 20. 11. 25. 28. 9. 11. 28. 25. 20. 14. 16. 28. 15. 10.
10. 20. 22. 15. 28. 17. 22. 24. 9. 26. 14. 28. 10. 9. 22.
8. 28. 11. 25.

KEY:

A neat code is to number the letters backwards, but you don't have to start with twenty-six. Try starting with a higher number. In this code, A equals twenty-eight.

A	= 28
B	= 27
C	= 26
D	= 25
E	= 24
F	= 23
G	= 22
H	= 21
I	= 20
J	= 19
K	= 18
L	= 17
M	= 16
N	= 15
O	= 14
P	= 13
Q	= 12
R	= 11
S	= 10
T	= 9
U	= 8
V	= 7
W	= 6
X	= 5
Y	= 4
Z	= 3

INCRIMINATING RECORDS

Fenton Hardy has been asked to serve as a witness in a very important case. Before the trial, he confides to his sons that he doesn't think his testimony will be enough to convict, and the police have been unable to find Augustine Frederick's records. "We must have those records," Fenton Hardy explains. "But I'm right in the middle of another case, and I can't follow it up."

The boys search Frederick's office, warehouse, yacht, home, and gardens. At one end of the garden is a greenhouse in which the man keeps rare and exotic tropical plants. "I'll bet it's somewhere in here," Frank says.

"Do you think he buried the records?" Joe asks.

Frank shrugs. Some time later, they find the records cleverly hidden behind huge brilliantly colored orchids.

Now they can deliver the evidence to their father, but he's working under cover and they can't contact him directly.

Posing as a delivery boy, Joe puts a coded note in a rolled up newspaper and places it in front of Mr. Hardy's door.

Can you help the ace detective read his sons' note?

RRNK4TLSIINSNTSDK   (1)

OIC1AIYTGSEACNOCZ   (9)

EDLE3RWTOVATSIGLX   (7)

CSOR1AAANEMRAOOUY   (8)

KEY:

Rearrange the numbers so that they are in their correct sequence—1 7 8 9, and write them down from left to right at the top of a page. Now arrange each row of letters (notice they are numbered) in a column under the corresponding number. Three meaningless letters have been added at the end. Read the message from left to right. Here is the first column:

1   7   8   9

R
R
N
K
4
T
L
S
I
I
N
S
N
T
S
D
K

THE BILLIONAIRE'S MESSAGE

Billionaire Jackson Rushton had been a recluse for the last twenty years, not even allowing members of his family to see him. He travels from country to country with his staff, taking entire floors of hotels.

After his death his will is read. It is simple and straightforward. As everyone expected, his entire family is disinherited, but they don't understand why.

"Dad walked out of the house one day," Jack Rushton, Jr. says. "We never knew what we had done, or why he left."

"But how can I help you now?" Fenton Hardy asks young Rushton.

"I'm not sure," Jack says. "I have a copy of the will here. There's some strange writing at the bottom. I don't mind being disinherited so much, but I wish I knew why."

Fenton Hardy studies the legal document. "This looks like a coded message at the bottom," he says. "My sons are experts at deciphering codes. I'll ask them to come in and help us."

Can you read the billionaire's message?

UA   RJ   RC   UC
SC   SO   ON   UJ   SS   UN   UO
RK   UA   RS   HN   TS   OA   TA   HK   UK   TN
UK   UN   UO   RN   HK   TC   OC
HS   TJ   TS   OA   TC
HS   TN   HK   RC   UC   OJ   HK   TS   TN   UK   TJ   HN
UA   OA   NJ   OC
TS   OJ   OK   TJ   OO   ON   UN   UO   HK   SS   UA   UO   RN
TK   UA   OJ   RC   UN   UO   SS   RS   SK   NJ
NC   TS   TN   UK

KEY:

	J	A	C	K	S	O	N
R	A	B	C	D	E	F	G
U	H	I/J	K	L	M	N	O
S	P	Q	R	S	T	U/V	W
H	X	Y	Z	A	B	C	D
T	E	F	G	H	I/J	K	L
O	M	N	O	P	Q	R	S
N	T	U/V	W	X	Y	Z	

STOLEN HEIRLOOMS

Mrs. Cornelia Simon-Smith is standing at the Hardys' front door, saying, "I simply must see him. He simply must help me."

"But he's not here," Mrs. Hardy explains. "My sons, Frank and Joe, often help him. Perhaps you would like to see them."

Mrs. Simon-Smith thinks for a moment. "This is highly confidential, you know," she explains to Mrs. Hardy.

Mrs. Hardy nods. "Of course."

Later, Mrs. Simon-Smith tells the boys that the family heirloom silver has been stolen. "My husband will never forgive me if he finds out," she explains.

"It's not your fault," Joe says.

Mrs. Simon-Smith looks down uncomfortably. "I gave a few pieces to a disreputable silversmith to repair and polish. He was inexpensive, you know. When he delivered them, he learned where all the silver was kept. My husband will say I was careless."

The boys take the case, and a short while later they discover the silver in the basement of the silversmith's shop, along with other valuable antique furniture and silver. While they are examining the heirlooms, they hear the sound of a door slamming. The basement has been locked!

The boys look for another exit, but they find only a small window several feet above them. They shout to attract attention, but there is no response. They know Chet and Biff will be looking for them shortly, but the silversmith may also be outside. They decide to write a coded note, which they attach to a weight with a rubber band and toss outside. Biff and Chet will find it. Can you help them read it?

31. 34. 13. 25. 15. 14. 24. 33. 12. 11. 43. 15. 32. 15. 33. 44.
52. 24. 44. 23. 43. 44. 34. 31. 15. 33. 11. 33. 44. 24. 41. 45.
15. 43. 13. 34. 33. 44. 11. 13. 44. 14. 11. 14.

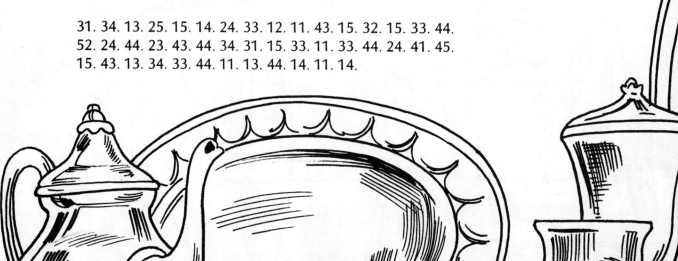

KEY:

One of the best ways to disguise a code is to keep the length of your words a secret. After you've substituted the correct letters for the numbers above, it will be easy to break them up into words.

LAND FRAUD

Paul and Amelia Holloway have just purchased some real estate from the Green Hills Land Corporation, only to discover that they have been cheated of their life savings. They had hoped to retire shortly, but now all their money is gone.

They ask the Hardys for help and the boys are sympathetic, but the real-estate dealer, Jake Pinchthorpe, has vanished.

"I guess there isn't much you can do for us, now," Paul Holloway says, "but we know that Jack Pinchthorpe has opened another business somewhere, and he's cheating somebody for sure.

The Hardys agree. "He's probably changed his name," Frank surmises.

"And his business," Joe adds. "But we'll find him."

And they do. But then they discover that Jake is part of a gang, and its members are closing in on them.

While the boys are seated in a restaurant, they notice that the gang members have surrounded them. "We'll never get out of here!" Frank says.

They decide to write a note to their dad. Then they address it and give it to the waiter with their check.

Though he is not sure of what is going on, the waiter senses the urgency of their request, and he sees to it that Fenton Hardy gets Frank and Joe's note.

Maybe you can help Mr. Hardy read it.

SRON EBPN HHRE AGNI LIEO EUCL URUD DYIC TOPG NIHL SDCM QIKY

KEY:

There are exactly forty-eight letters in this code. Divide the letters in half so that you have two lines of twenty-four characters each. Starting with the top row, take one letter at a time from each row and combine them. The first word in this code is "surrounded." That should help you to figure out the rest.

CORRUPT CANDIDATE

Monty Mulligan, a clever and unscrupulous man, has decided to run for mayor of Bayport. Fenton Hardy, who knows the man is corrupt, tells his sons, "We must stop him!"

Frank and Joe offer to work as volunteers at Monty's campaign headquarters, where they learn that the man plans to tamper with the voting machines.

Not wanting to arouse suspicion, the boys continue to work, but first they must send their dad a message. If the mayoral candidate is caught red-handed, it will end his political career.

Chet, who has been helping the Hardys, comes in every afternoon with a coffee delivery.

"We'll give him a note," Frank says.

The boys write their note, but they use a code just in case anyone stops their friend. Then, when Chet is on his way out, Joe slips him the coded note.

If you were Fenton Hardy, would you be able to help the boys?

MOSIW   OTMGA   NIIHR   TNDTE   YGNMH   FMIEO
IAGEU   XCHTS   IHTUE   NITSZ   GNOAZ   VENTZ

KEY:

Count the number of letters in this message. There are sixty. If you use a grid with five rows down and twelve across, that will give you the right number of spaces. Now arrange your letters in columns, starting with the first group of five letters. The grid should help. We'll start deciphering the code for you.

	1	2	3	4	5	6	7	8	9	10	11	12
1	M											
2	O											
3	S											
4	I											
5	W											

FRAUDULENT STOCKS

Frank and Joe Hardy are working under cover in the offices of Bagelman and Bagelman. The two men have been selling stocks for an imaginary gold mine out West, but they are not working alone. And Fenton Hardy wants the whole gang.

Mr. Hardy goes out West to investigate, while the boys stay in the small New York office and learn exactly how the whole operation works.

One day, while Joe is trailing one of the accomplices, Frank notices that Bagelman is leaving the office with a large suitcase.

"I'll bet that's money he's carrying. . .and the fake stock," Frank tells himself.

Several of the men are in the office, but Frank decides he must follow Bagelman. He writes a note on Joe's desk calendar, and just to make sure that none of the men will suspect him, Frank writes it in code.

Can you help Joe read the message?

7. 6. 12. 10. 17. 18. 6. 19. 23. 26. 19. 19. 14. 19. 12.
20. 26. 25. 28. 14. 25. 13. 18. 20. 19. 10. 30. 6. 19. 9.
11. 6. 16. 10. 24. 25. 20. 8. 16. 24. 28. 14. 17. 17. 11.
20. 17. 17. 20. 28. 8. 6. 17. 17. 30. 20. 26. 17. 6. 25. 10. 23.

KEY:

When you are substituting numbers for letters, there's no rule that says you have to start with 1. Here we are starting with the number 6 as A. The rest is easy. After you get the correct letters, separate them into words. Expert cryptographers like to disguise the length of their words.

A	=	6
B	=	7
C	=	8
D	=	9
E	=	10
F	=	11
G	=	12
H	=	13
I	=	14
J	=	15
K	=	16
L	=	17
M	=	18
N	=	19
O	=	20
P	=	21
Q	=	22
R	=	23
S	=	24
T	=	25
U	=	26
V	=	27
W	=	28
X	=	29
Y	=	30
Z	=	31

THE SEARCH FOR LORENA BELL

Young Lorena Bell has disappeared. Her father is desperate, her mother half out of her mind with worry. Then they receive a ransom note.

Fenton Hardy has been asked to take the case. The Bells are willing to pay the ransom, but they are fearful for Lorena's safety.

The Hardy's interview the household help, and they develop a theory as to where Lorena is. They think she may be somewhere in New York City. Mr. Hardy investigates to see if he can find any more clues.

"I'll be in touch with you," he tells the boys. "Be ready to help at a moment's notice."

One day, while Frank is reading the Bayport paper, something on the sports page catches his attention. "Look at this small display ad," he says to Joe.

"I can't make it out." Joe seems puzzled.

"Of course not," Frank says. "I think it's in code, and I'll bet it's from Dad."

Can you help the boys decipher this one? It's important.

ANNKLETEATTN EDLOYIOMAMOV LHSECAIATPEE
NILRFMRETOUE OEMWITMNMELS RLAYTTPTEXRE

KEY:

Make six columns, each having twelve lines. Now write the name Lorena in the spaces across the top. If you look carefully at the coded message, you will notice that each series of twelve letters begins with a letter from the name Lorena. In the first column, write all the letters following the "L" in the coded message. In the second, write all the letters following the "O". Continue to follow this procedure until you have filled in all the spaces. Now read each line from left to right, and you will have a message from Mr. Hardy. We'll start for you. You do the rest.

L
H
S
E
C
A
I
A
T
P
E
E

BAYPORT NEWS

LAB THEFT

The laboratories of Binny and Finny have been doing some very important research, which will one day have far-reaching effects. Dr. Binny calls Fenton Hardy and explains that someone has stolen their results. This is a disaster!

Mr. Hardy checks the backgrounds of current and former employees, while Frank and Joe join the organization as lab assistants to Dr. Binny.

For the first week, the boys notice nothing unusual, but one morning when they report for work, they realize that someone has been tampering with the files.

Late that night Frank returns to the lab, while Joe conducts a search of the apartment of Elias Holden, an employee whose behavior has been very strange.

Frank moves around the lab very quietly, especially when he realizes that someone else is also there. Then he sees Holden close a file and start to leave the lab. Frank decides to follow, but first he must leave a note for Joe, just in case Joe comes to the lab to look for him.

To make sure that Holden's fellow conspirators can't read the note, he decides to write it in code.

TLDEF AOELI IHNOL LGHTE INESS

KEY:

Write each letter as you come to it in the grid below, from left to right as you would normally read it. After doing this, you can read the message by reading down the first column, up the next, down the third, and so on.

THE HIDDEN NOTE

A beautiful sculpture is on its way from Florence, Italy, to the United States, on loan to a prestigious New York museum. The museum director calls Frank and Joe, and tells them that menacing calls have been coming in. Someone is threatening to destroy the sculpture.

"You know that priceless, irreplaceable works of art have been destroyed by vandals in Europe. We don't want it to happen here," the museum director explains.

Frank and Joe vow that nothing will happen to the masterpiece. The boys check out the museum day after day, looking for clues and watching visitors.

One day they see a checkroom attendant place a note in a checked shopping bag. Joe surreptitiously takes the note and looks at it. It's in code. Can you help Frank and Joe identify the culprits?

READY PLAN WE CREATE TEN AUTHORITIES TO EVERYONE CAN COMMOTION SHARP BUSY GO WATCHING STEAL NEAR TOMORROW FOR ON SCULPTURE THE SCULPTURE MORNING ONE GAME NOW REMBRANDT AT KEEP HOUR

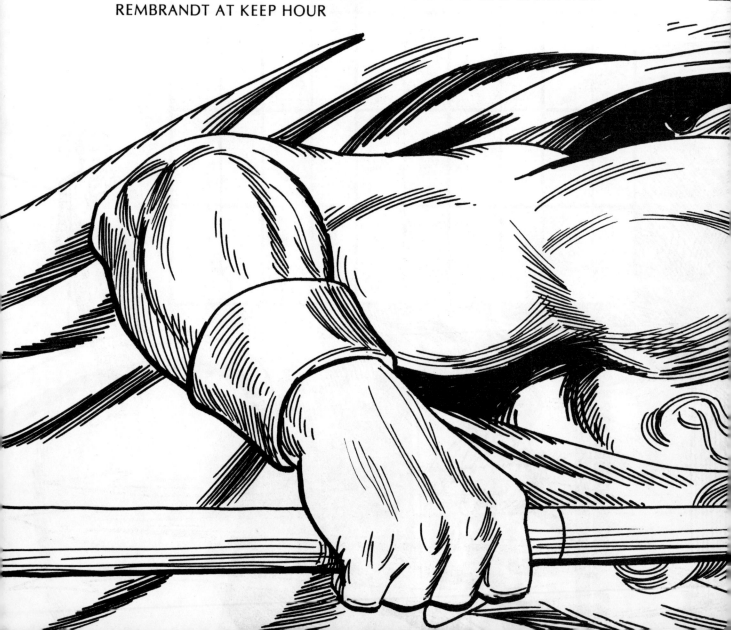

KEY:

There are thirty words in this message. The easiest way to decipher it is to use a grid like the one below, which is five spaces wide and six spaces deep. Put your first six words in the first column, then put the second six words in the next column, and so on. When you have placed all the words in the correct order, read the message from left to right, as you would normally. We'll fill in the first column. You can do the rest.

READY				
PLAN				
WE				
CREATE				
TEN				
AUTHORITIES				

GOLD HEIST

The local TV station is featuring a documentary on gold. As a part of their advertising for the program they have announced that they plan to have a million dollars worth of gold bullion right there at their offices. On the morning of the show an armored truck rolls into town with the gold.

The boys are watching the program with Aunt Gertrude. She is fascinated by the stacks of gold bricks.

"Don't you think," she says to them, "that they're taking foolish chances, bringing a million dollars in bullion to the station."

"Oh, Aunt Gertrude. You worry too much," Joe tells her.

Frank remarks, "The announcer looks very uncomfortable."

Just then the narrator announces, "Anyone who wants more information should contact the U.S. Treasury Department." He goes on to give the address.

Something flashes on the screen. At first the boys think it is the address of the United States Treasury Department, but suddenly realize it is a coded message.

Quickly, they take pencil and paper and write the message down. Can you help them decipher it?

ENSA BLXW AJAM XANA LQML AETY
QTBD KTTW QRMA RBPQ TWCA

KEY:

To confuse anyone who shouldn't read this code, the message is divided into four-letter units. But it will be easy to read once you have the key. Just substitute the correct letters for the cipher letters, then separate the characters into words.

A B C D E F G H I J K L M N O P Q R S T U V W X Y Z
E D C B A Z Y X W V U T S R Q P O N M L K J I H G F

THE BIG BET

Chet, Biff, Tony, and Frank and Joe Hardy have taken their dates to the big football game of the year.

They are all excited, since they have been looking forward to this game for months. Just as they are taking their seats, Joe looks up and recognizes an underworld figure.

"What do you think he's doing here?" he asks Frank.

"I don't know, but I think it's a bad sign."

"I'm going to tail him," Joe says.

Frank agrees. "Okay. While you tail Slick Mickie, I'll keep my eyes open."

Frank begins to feel very uncomfortable, and when he sees the players come out of the locker rooms, he notices that one of the Polecat players looks very familiar. Now he's really worried.

Then a vendor hands Frank a hot dog in which he has cleverly hidden a note. It's from Joe, and in code. Can you help Frank decipher it?

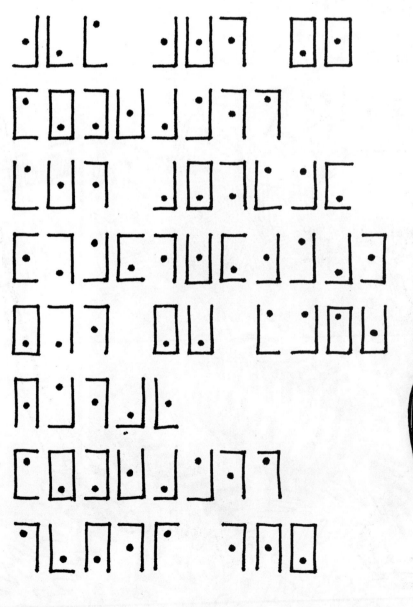

KEY:

A •	D •	G •
B •	E •	H •
C •	F •	I •
J •	M •	P •
K •	N •	Q •
L •	O •	R •
S •	V •	Y •
T •	W •	Z •
U •	X •	

DANGER IN THE CORAL REEFS

Frank, Joe, Biff, Tony, and Chet are bound for Australia to deliver important documents to the American ambassador there. They call Ambassador Drake the minute their plane lands, only to learn that he will be gone for a few days. The boys are disappointed, especially since they have been instructed to give the papers to no one but the ambassador.

Nevertheless, there is a great deal the boys want to do. They decide to see the beautiful Australian coral reef. Just to be sure nothing happens to the documents, Frank and Joe each take some, put them in plastic bags, and tape them under their wetsuits. Then they go scuba diving.

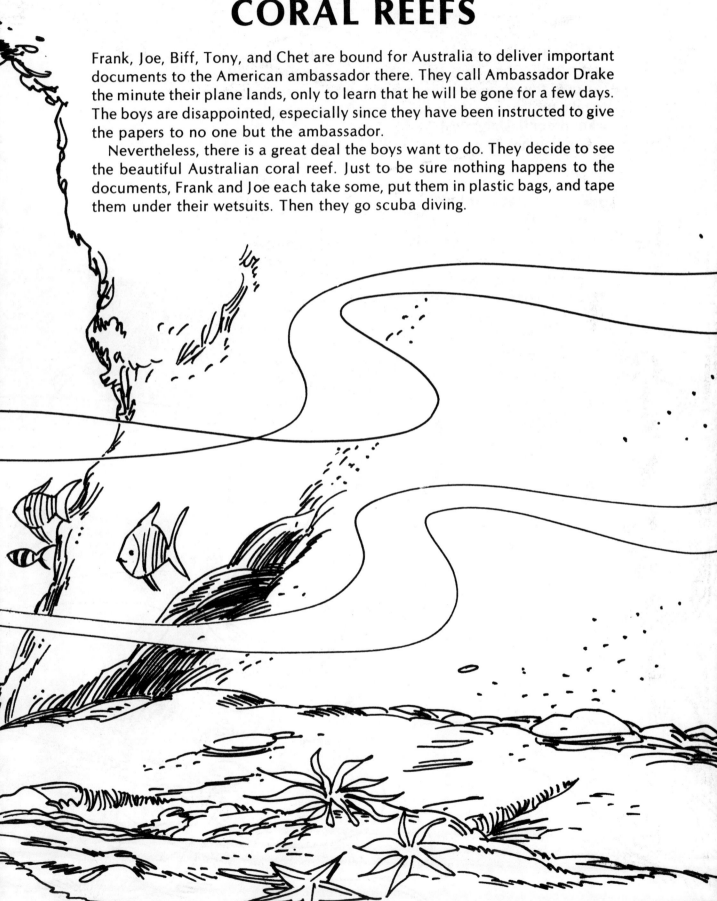

After a while, Joe notices that he has become separated from his brother and friends. Then he realizes that he is being followed.

Could this be an enemy? Someone who wants the documents? Joe decides to take no chances. He must get help. He slips behind some coral, takes out a waterproof flashlight, and sends a signal.

Can you help Frank read Joe's message?

●●●/ ━ ━ ━/ ●●●/
━●●●/ ●/ ●●/ ━●/ ━ ━●/
●●━●/ ━ ━ ━/ ●━●●/ ●━●●/ ━ ━ ━/ ●━ ━/ ●/ ━●●/
━●●●/ ━●━ ━/
●/ ━●/ ●/ ━ ━/ ━●━ ━/
●●●/ ●━ ━/ ●●/ ━ ━/ ━ ━/ ●/ ●━●/
━●━●/ ━ ━ ━/ ━ ━/ ●/
━ ━●━/ ●●━/ ●●/ ━●━●/ ━●━/
●●●/ ━ ━ ━/ ●●●/

KEY:

A •—
B —•••
C —•—•
D —••
E •
F ••—•
G ——•

H ••••
I ••
J •———
K —•—
L •—••
M ——
N —•

O ———
P •——•
Q ——•—
R •—•
S •••
T —
U ••—

V •••—
W •——
X —••—
Y —•——
Z ——••

LETTER FROM AN OLD FRIEND

Aunt Gertrude has just received a letter from an old friend who has spent the last five years in a nursing home. Though the letter seems cheerful, Aunt Gertrude has doubts.

"I've been wondering what happened to her all these years," Aunt Gertrude says. "I don't know why Ellen would go to a nursing home, though. She was always so active and healthy."

"She probably didn't want to manage a large house," Fenton Hardy suggests.

"But she loved it," Aunt Gertrude replies. "She had a beautiful ranch with stables, and enjoyed every minute of her life. She has no immediate family, but her cousins were always taking advantage of her."

Mr. Hardy shrugs. "I'm sure she's all right," he says.

"Guess you're right," Aunt Gertrude agrees. "But I wish I could be sure. Maybe I'll visit her sometime."

After a while Aunt Gertrude examines the note more closely. "I wonder why some of these letters look darker than the others," she says to her nephews.

"Let's see," Frank Hardy replies.

He and Joe scrutinize the letter carefully.

"Do you see what I see?" Joe asks his brother.

"You bet," Frank answers. "Aunt Gertrude, you could be right, after all. We'll be back in a minute, after we figure this out."

Can you guess what the boys see?

DEAR GERTRUDE,
  IT HAS **BEEN** MORE THAN FIVE YEARS S**IN**CE I LAST SAW YOU, BUT I HAVE THO**UG**HT OF YOU OFTEN.
  I AM STAYING AT A NURSING **H**OME IN ROS**EVIL**LE. A WON**D**ERFUL PLACE.
  WE **H**AVE **G**RAND TIMES, AND **SO** I HAVE LI**TT**LE TIME TO WRITE.
  BUT YOU ARE ONE OF **MY** GOOD FRIENDS, AND I **W**ANTED TO KNOW WHAT YOU ARE DOING AND WHETHER YOU ARE WE**LL**.
  HEARING FROM YOU WOULD BE WONDERFUL. **P**LEASE WRITE!
  WE ALL LOOK FOR **C**ORRESP**ON**DENCE. **IT** **M**A**K**ES US **C**HEERFUL **AT** THE BEGINNING OF

THE DAY.
  YOU WILL BE SURPRISED TO GET **MY** **L**ETTER, BUT I HOPE YOU'LL BE PLE**A**SED TO HEAR FROM ME, AND **W**RITE VER**Y** SOON. I'LL ANSW**ER** PROMPTLY.
  THEN I CAN TELL YOU ALL ABOUT THIS **PL**ACE AND HOW **EN**JO**YA**BLE IT HAS BEEN DURING THE LA**ST** FIV**E** YEARS.

LOVE,
Ellen

HUNT FOR THE HARRISON BAND

Fenton Hardy has been on a top-secret assignment for six months. He is closing in on the Harrison Band, bank robbers who have stolen enormous sums of money and negotiable bonds from ten banks on the East Coast.

Frank and Joe know that at any time their father may need help.

One day, while they are walking down the street in Bayport, they are confronted by a young man who is passing out fliers advertising a recently opened restaurant.

He holds out a sheet to Frank and another to Joe, and the look in his eye warns the boys to accept the advertisements.

"There's nothing on here that should interest us," Joe says.

"Look at the back," Frank tells him.

"Nothing here but some dots."

"He handed me something too, Frank says. "Let's see what it is." He turns the slip over and sees the alphabet.

"We'd better decipher this fast," Joe says as he looks over his brother's shoulder. "It must be a message from Dad."

What did Mr. Hardy ask the boys to do?

KEY:

Mr. Hardy used a clever trick. He gave the boys his coded message in two parts. Joe got the sheet with the dots. Frank was given the alphabet. After a few experiments, the boys knew how to put it all together so that it would work. We've done that step for you. Now all you have to do is to write down the letter corresponding to each dot, starting from the top and working your way down. The first word is "Harrison." Can you decipher the rest?

A	B	C	D	E	F	G	H	I	J	K	L	M	N	O	P	Q	R	S	T	U	V	W	X	Y	Z	#
							•																			1
•																										2
																	•									3
																	•									4
								•																		5
																		•								6
														•												7
													•													8
							•																			9
				•																						10
•																										11
			•																							12
																•										13
																				•						14
•																										15
																	•									16
																			•							17
				•																						18
																	•									19
																		•								20
								•																		21
													•													22
											•															23
•																										24
																						•				25
																	•									26
				•																						27
													•													28
		•																								29
				•																						30
												•														31
				•																						32
				•																						33
																			•							34
												•														35
				•																						36
•																										37
																			•							38
																		•								39
												•														40
								•																		41
																			•							42
							•																			43
•																										44
													•													45
			•																							46
																					•					47
								•																		48
													•													49
				•																						50
																			•							51
				•																						52
													•													53
																			•							54
														•												55
													•													56
								•																		57
						•																				58
							•																			59
																			•							60

WASHINGTON HOTLINE

Frank and Joe Hardy are waiting for their dad at the Bayport Airport when they hear a commotion on the airfield. A man with a briefcase is standing between two men with guns. He looks frightened and uncomfortable.

The boys realize that the man is being kidnapped. They slip into a locker room, put on work clothes, and manage to get on the field, where they pretend they are part of the crew preparing the plane the kidnappers have commandeered.

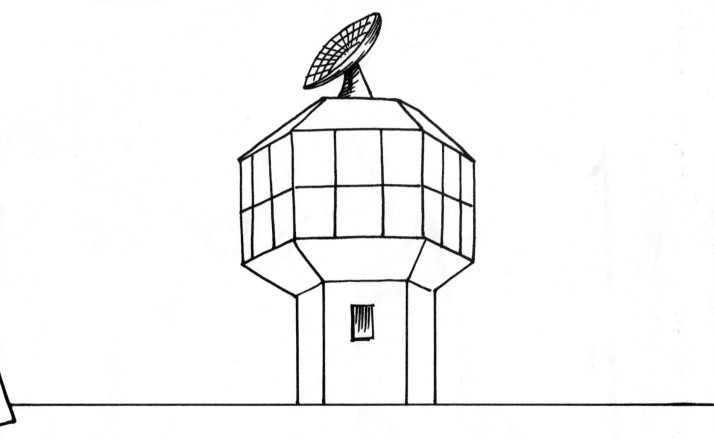

As the man is being dragged to the craft, Frank sees him drop something. The boy picks it up. "Joe, this looks like a note—and it's in code. He must have written this before he was kidnapped."

NMAY WMZI SDAP WMJM ACDQ FDYJ NMZA WFYW
TTZY UBJT MADB ADJP BJUH DDOB KHOM LDIM
QIDL DALM JWTF WFDH IMAT BYND HQRV

KEY: DOCUMENTS

E	F	G	H	I	J	K	L	M	N	O	P	Q	R	S	T	U	V	W	X	Y	Z	A	B	C	D
D	O	C	U	M	E	N	T	S	A	B	F	G	H	I	J	K	L	P	Q	R	V	W	X	Y	Z

This is a bit tricky, but it's easy once you get the hang of it. The first line is the alphabet, but it has been shifted so that it starts with E. Normally, E would be A. But to make it more difficult to decipher, a double substitution is used. The letters in the word "documents" are substituted for the first nine letters of the transposed alphabet, then the remaining letters of the alphabet follow. If you have the key, deciphering the code is the same in any case, just substitute the letters in the first row for corresponding letters in the second row. Three meaningless letters have been added at the end.

STRANDED!

Frank and Joe learn that poachers are operating on one of the Thousand Islands in the St. Lawrence River. They decide to investigate, conducting a search of the uninhabited islands. Finally they find what they have been looking for. . .a cache of illegally obtained sealskins.

Just as they pick up some of the evidence to take back to the boat, they hear a noise. Someone has cut their boat loose. They see a man in a motorboat and call out to him, but he just waves and laughs.

"Now maybe you Hardys will stay off my back!" he calls out.

"Well," Joe says, "I guess we're stranded."

Frank says, "Our friends Chet, Biff, and Tony will look for us if we don't turn up soon, so let's get ready to signal them."

They take out their semaphore flags and start working out their message. Can you help the Hardys friends decipher it?

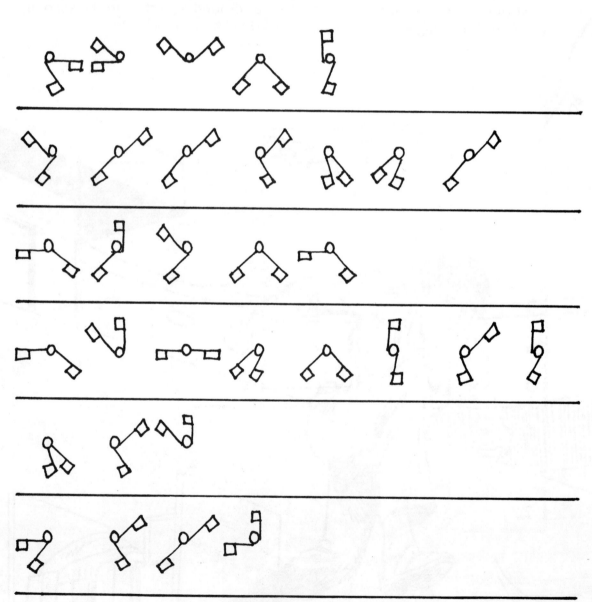

KEY:

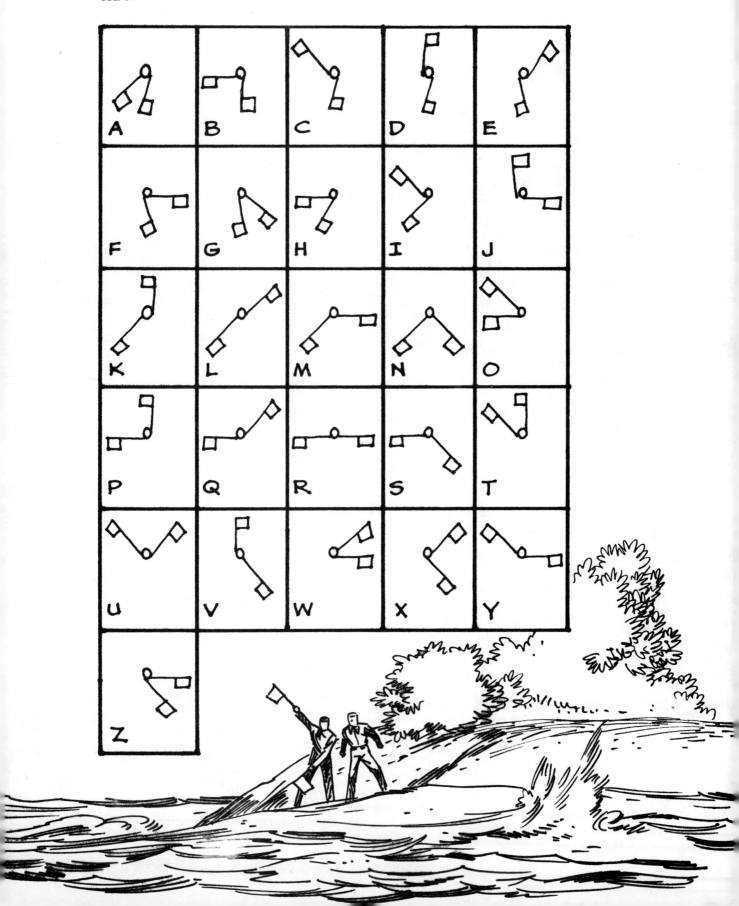

MESSAGE FROM THE PAST

During a bicycle trip through England and Scotland, Frank and Joe Hardy stop in a small village located at the foot of an old castle in the Scottish Highlands. The boys plan to stay at a local inn for the night. While they are seated at a small table in the dark, picturesque dining room, they hear Peers, the innkeeper, speaking with some of the villagers.

"You planning to keep a lookout tonight?" he asks.

"Not me!" one of the men says. "Constable went up today."

"Have you seen him since?" another asks.

The men shake their heads.

Intrigued, the Hardys later ask Peers if something is wrong.

He confides that something strange is going on in the castle. "Don't know what to do about Constable," he adds.

The boys offer to go to the castle and look for the officer if the innkeeper will act as a guide. He agrees, but reluctantly.

Peers leads them to the castle, up and down winding staircases, through long narrow tunnels, and into rooms that look like cells. Finally they come to a large underground chamber. Constable is lying on the floor. He has been hit on the head. In the far corner is a sarcaphogus. The Hardys can see that it's been tampered with. Then they notice something else. There are marks on it, which look like part of a code that the boys recognize. Can you help them decipher the code?

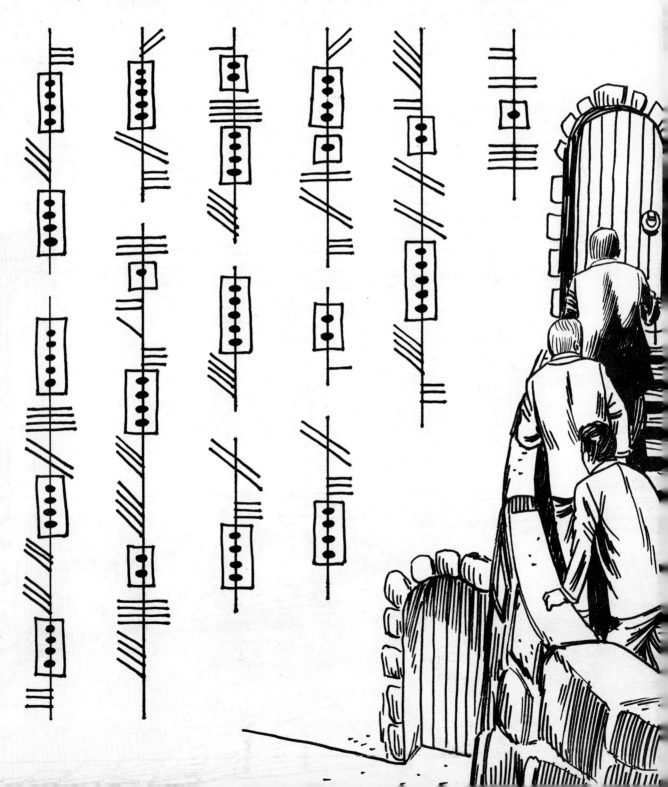

KEY:

CATCHING UP WITH RAWSON'S GANG

"I don't know what's going on anymore," Mrs. Hardy says to her sons. "A guru and his followers have moved into the house on Senator Street. You should see how they dress."

The boys are amused. "Variety is the spice of life," Joe tells her.

"Hmph," Aunt Gertrude snorts. "They're too permissive. That's what I say. They have a little ceremony on the lawn at dawn every day."

That evening the boys learn that the New York police are looking for Homer Rawson after finding a cache of guns, bombs, and ammunition in his apartment.

A short while later, they receive a phone call from their dad. "The police think the Rawson gang is in Bayport."

"Gang?" Joe asks.

"Yes," Mr. Hardy replies. "They all lived in an apartment in New York and collected guns and made bombs."

"Why do the police suspect they're in Bayport?" Frank asks.

"Their car was abandoned on Bayport Road," Mr. Hardy explains.

The boys wonder whether the guru and his friends are really the Rawson gang.

"Let's go to the guru's house, Joe," Frank says. "If Rawson's there, it won't take us long to find out."

And it doesn't. After a brief search, the boys find weapons, ammunition, and a diary, but the diary is written in code. Can you help Frank and Joe read one of its entries?

CBYV PRSB HAQU VQRB HGWH FGOR SBER FGEV
ZRAH FGFG NEGN TNVA GURJ BEYQ JVYY XABJ
BSBH ECYV TUGK

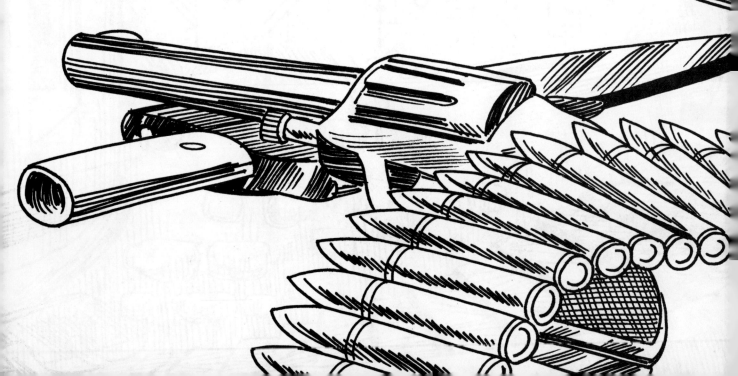

A	B	C	D	E	F	G	H	I	J	K	L	M	N	O	P	Q	R	S	T	U	V	W	X	Y	Z
N	O	P	Q	R	S	T	U	V	W	X	Y	Z	A	B	C	D	E	F	G	H	I	J	K	L	M

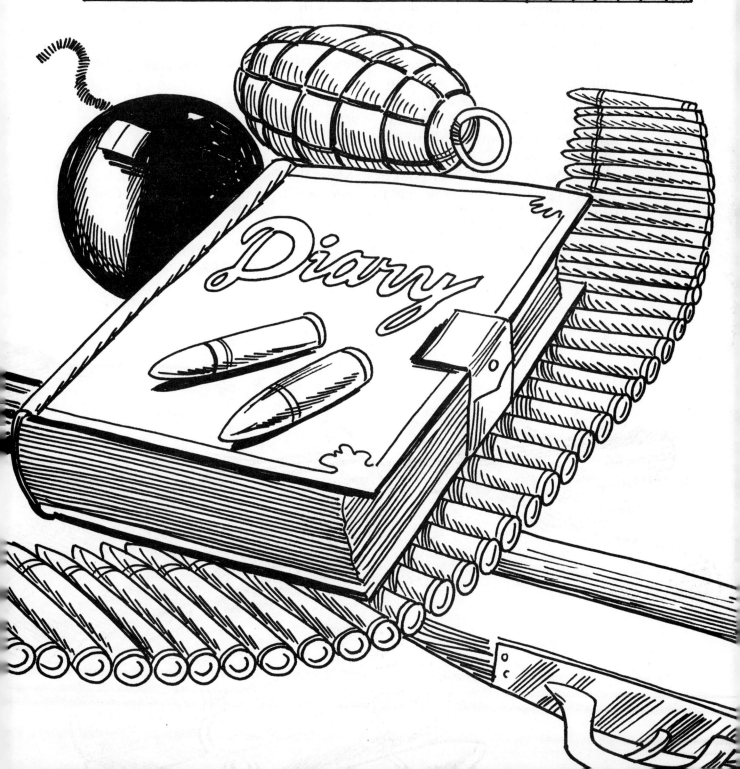

ABA BABA'S CROWN

The crown of Aba Baba has been stolen. Each gem in it is priceless, and it has been passed down from father to son for countless generations.

Aba Baba visits Fenton Hardy. "You must help me," he says. "I rule a superstitious country. If the people learn about this theft, they will believe my reign has lost the sanction of the gods. This cannot be good. I fear bloodshed."

Mr. Hardy agrees to help Aba Baba. He learns that a cousin, Abu Ben Vudu, wants to take over Aba Baba's small kingdom and is hiding out in Los Angeles with the crown. At the proper time the man will appear before the people at the head of an army—with the crown.

He must be stopped! Mr. Hardy goes under cover. He opens a small fortune teller's shop near Ben Vudu's hideout. The boys, in disguise, go to the shop to discuss the case with him.

One day, when Frank and Joe visit Mr. Hardy, the doors are locked. "Dad's gone off somewhere," Frank says. "Wish we knew where! I'll bet it has something to do with Aba Baba's crown."

"Wait," Joe says. "Do you see what I see?"

Frank looks down. Sticking out from under the door is the corner of a note. The boys pick it up and look at it. It's a message from their dad, in code. Can you help them read it?

BENR ERAT NTRH VOMR URSE DEME UCET OEEH
NITR WVME AEEE YSAT TTTH OOPR PLIE IEEE

KEY: 16 x 4

Since the key is 16 x 4, you know you have sixteen four-letter groups. To decipher, write the first four letters from left to right, then write the second underneath. Go on writing down all the letters until you have sixteen four-letter series. Then, going from the top down and from left to right, write down each letter. Now you can separate the letters into words.

ANSWERS:

1) Flight by Caravan
Spotted by Federation spy. Must leave. Will call you.

2) Midsummer Night
Warburton's life in danger. Must leave theater. Get us out of Smith Building.

3) Greenhouse Front
I am locked in cell under greenhouse.

4) The Lost Scroll
Placed scroll in clay reproduction of Venus figurine.

5) Danger on the Ski Slopes
Lodge sabotaged by Gordon. Employees bribed. Need help to close in.
Being watched.

6) The Great Whale Hunt
Poachers trail *Sea Bird* at radioman's signal. Get Coast Guard.

7) Incriminating Records
Records in locker 1431 at railway station. Gives names, transactions.
Good luck.

8) The Billionaire's Message
Jack Rushton died in fall long ago. Being blackmailed into impersonating
him. Contest will.

9) Stolen Heirlooms
Locked in basement with stolen antiques. Contact Dad.

10) Land Fraud
Surrounded by Pinchthorpe gang in Hillside. Come quick.

11) Corrupt Candidate
Monty fixing voting machines midnight tonight. Meet us at warehouse.

12) Fraudulent Stocks
Bagelman running out with money and fake stocks. Will follow.
Call you later.

13) The Search for Lorena Bell
Lorena held in small New York City flat. Time important. Meet me at Apex
Motel, Route seven.

14) Lab Theft
Tailing Holden. He stole files.

15) The Hidden Note
Ready to go on game plan. Everyone watching sculpture. Now we can steal the Rembrandt. Create commotion near sculpture at ten sharp tomorrow morning. Keep authorities busy for one hour.

16) Gold Heist
Armed thieves here to steal gold bullion. Send police.

17) The Big Bet
Big bet on Polecats. Get Cougar quarterback out of game. Watch Polecats sixty-two.

18) Danger in the Coral Reefs
S.O.S. Being followed by enemy swimmer. Come quick. S.O.S.

19) Letter from an Old Friend
Being held against my will. Help. Contact my lawyer. Please.

20) Hunt for the Harrison Band
Harrison headquarters in Lawrence. Meet me at Smith and Vine ten tonight.

21) Washington Hotline
Kincaid's men waiting. Expect kidnap. Call D.C. hotline one-two-three-four-five-six-seven. Vital papers in locker.

22) Stranded
Found illegal skins. Stranded. Get help.

23) Message From the Past
Here interred with MacPherson's bones is the wealth of the Scottish clan.

24) Catching Up With Rawson's Gang
Police found hideout just before strike. Must start again. The world will know of our plight.

25) Aba Baba's Crown
Ben Vudu on way to pier to receive stolen arms. Meet me at Pier three-three-three.

ORDER FORM

HARDY BOYS™
MYSTERY STORIES
by Franklin W. Dixon

Now that you've met Frank and Joe Hardy, we're sure you'll want to read the thrilling books in the *Hardy Boys*™ adventure series.

To make it easy for you to own all the books in this exciting series, we've enclosed this handy order form.

57 TITLES AT YOUR BOOKSELLER OR COMPLETE THIS HANDY COUPON AND MAIL TO:

GROSSET & DUNLAP, INC.
P.O. Box 941, Madison Square Post Office, New York, N.Y. 10010

Please send me the *Hardy Boys*™ *Mystery Stories* checked below @ $2.95 each, plus 25¢ *per book* postage and handling. My check or money order for $_____ is enclosed. (Please *do not* send cash.)

☐ 1.	Tower Treasure	8901-7	
☐ 2.	House on the Cliff	8902-5	
☐ 3.	Secret of the Old Mill	8903-3	
☐ 4.	Missing Chums	8904-1	
☐ 5.	Hunting for Hidden Gold	8905-X	
☐ 6.	Shore Road Mystery	8906-8	
☐ 7.	Secret of the Caves	8907-6	
☐ 8.	Mystery of Cabin Island	8908-4	
☐ 9.	Great Airport Mystery	8909-2	
☐ 10.	What Happened At Midnight	8910-6	
☐ 11.	While the Clock Ticked	8911-4	
☐ 12.	Footprints Under the Window	8912-2	
☐ 13.	Mark on the Door	8913-0	
☐ 14.	Hidden Harbor Mystery	8914-9	
☐ 15.	Sinister Sign Post	8915-7	
☐ 16.	A Figure in Hiding	8916-6	
☐ 17.	Secret Warning	8917-3	
☐ 18.	Twisted Claw	8918-1	
☐ 19.	Disappearing Floor	8919-X	
☐ 20.	Mystery of the Flying Express	8920-3	
☐ 21.	The Clue of the Broken Blade	8921-1	
☐ 22.	The Flickering Torch Mystery	8922-X	
☐ 23.	Melted Coins	8923-3	
☐ 24.	Short-Wave Mystery	8924-6	
☐ 25.	Secret Panel	8925-4	
☐ 26.	The Phantom Freighter	8926-2	
☐ 27.	Secret of Skull Mountain	8927-0	
☐ 28.	The Sign of the Crooked Arrow	8928-9	

☐ 29.	The Secret of the Lost Tunnel	8929-7
☐ 30.	Wailing Siren Mystery	8930-0
☐ 31.	Secret of Wildcat Swamp	8931-9
☐ 32.	Crisscross Shadow	8932-7
☐ 33.	The Yellow Feather Mystery	8933-5
☐ 34.	The Hooded Hawk Mystery	8934-3
☐ 35.	The Clue in the Embers	8935-1
☐ 36.	The Secrets of Pirates Hill	8936-X
☐ 37.	Ghost at Skeleton Rock	8937-8
☐ 38.	Mystery at Devil's Paw	8938-6
☐ 39.	Mystery of the Chinese Junk	8939-4
☐ 40.	Mystery of the Desert Giant	8940-8
☐ 41.	Clue of the Screeching Owl	8941-6
☐ 42.	Viking Symbol Mystery	8942-4
☐ 43.	Mystery of the Aztec Warrior	8943-2
☐ 44.	Haunted Fort	8944-0
☐ 45.	Mystery of the Spiral Bridge	8945-9
☐ 46.	Secret Agent on Flight 101	8946-7
☐ 47.	Mystery of the Whale Tattoo	8947-5
☐ 48.	The Arctic Patrol Mystery	8948-3
☐ 49.	The Bombay Boomerang	8949-1
☐ 50.	Danger on Vampire Trail	8950-5
☐ 51.	The Masked Monkey	8951-3
☐ 52.	The Shattered Helmet	8952-3
☐ 53.	The Clue of the Hissing Serpent	8953-X
☐ 54.	The Mysterious Caravan	8954-8
☐ 55.	The Witchmaster's Key	8955-6
☐ 56.	The Jungle Pyramid	8956-4
☐ 57.	The Firebird Rocket	8957-2

SHIP TO:

NAME _____
(please print)

ADDRESS _____

CITY _____ STATE _____ ZIP _____

Printed in U.S.A.

Please do not send cash.